D0435621

This Ladybird Book belongs to:

_____

_____

_____

_____

Published by Penguin Books India
11 Community Centre, Panchsheel Park, New Delhi 110017

© PENGUIN BOOKS INDIA LTD 2005
1 3 5 7 9 10 8 6 4 2

Printed in Ajanta Offset, New Delhi

The Grateful Parrot

This Ladybird retelling by
MEERA UBEROI

illustrated
by
TAPOSHI GHOSHAL

based on a story from the Jataka Tales

One day, Indra, the king of heaven, was sitting in his throne. As usual, he was being grumpy. He complained to his wife Indrani, 'The creatures on earth are not grateful. They always ask me for more and more, but they never appreciate what anyone has done for them.'

'That is not true!' said Indrani. 'Have you not seen the parrot king?'

And Indra looked down from heaven to see what was happening with the parrot king.

On the banks of the Ganga, where the river curves and bends, there stood a beautiful fig tree. It was a tall and strong tree, and it was the only tree for many miles. In it lived the parrot king and his flock of one thousand birds.

The parrot king loved this tree dearly. He had been born in it and had lived in it all his life. He ate fruit from only that tree. His flock ate the fruit of the tree too and drank water from the river that flowed by it.

'So this is him,' said Indra. 'Hmm, lets see how good he really is!'

He waved his hand over the great, beautiful tree. It began to lose its fruit and leaves.

The flock of parrots exclaimed in horror and shock for a couple of hours. But after that they became hungry, so they flew down the river to where there were other fig trees. They made their new homes there.

All except one bird.

The parrot king continued to stay in his old tree. As the last leaves fell off, he told the tree, 'I will never leave you. You sheltered me when I was a baby, you fed me and gave me a home all my life. I will never leave you, now that an ill wind has blown over you.'

As there were no fruits left on the branches, the parrot ate the ones that lay on the ground beneath.

When these too were gone, he survived by drinking the water of the river.

When he became too weak to fly, he lay down against the trunk of the tree. 'I will never leave you,' he murmured, 'in good times and bad!'

In heaven, Indra was stunned. 'What gratitude! What faithfulness!' he exclaimed. 'But I wonder how long it will last!'

Days went by. The parrot grew weaker and weaker. The day came when he knew he was dying. 'I won't leave you, even to save my life,' he said, looking up at the leafless branches.

Indra could not believe his eyes. 'This parrot is too good to be true,' he said.

Indra turned himself into a swan and flew down to the fig tree.

'Oh parrot!' he said. 'Why do you stay with this dead tree? Birds always leave dead trees!'

'Hello swan!' said the parrot weakly. 'I stay with this tree because it has always fed me and sheltered me. Should I leave it now that it has lost its leaves and fruit?'

'Of course,' said the swan. 'Trees die, birds leave. That's the way it is. Do you want to die too?'

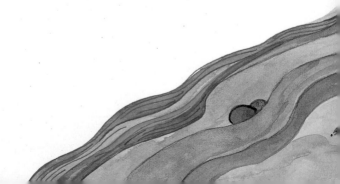

'No, I don't,' said the parrot. 'But I stayed with it in good times. I would be the most ungrateful creature on earth if I left it now.'

The swan beamed in delight. 'Well said! If you had one wish that could come true, what would you ask for?'

'I would ask that this tree live again. Let the sap run through its mighty trunk and cover its branches with glossy green leaves,' said the parrot.

As the words left his red beak, there was a loud clap of thunder. The swan vanished and in its place stood Indra.

The parrot tried to rise but Indra gently pressed him back. 'Stay where you are!' he said.

He pointed to the river. A sparkling fountain rose up and rained down on the tree.

In the blink of an eye, the tree
stood tall and proud, its branches
covered with rustling leaves and
honey-sweet fruit.

There were tears of joy on the parrot's
face. 'How can I thank you, my lord?'
he asked.

'There is no need for thanks,'
said Indra gently. 'I tested you
and found you worthy.'
He vanished in a flash.

The parrot flew up into the leafy branches, lovingly brushing them with his wings. 'Ah my tree!' he sighed. 'I am so happy to be within your branches again.'

The leaves rustled and whispered, and a branch dipped down to touch the parrot as he fell asleep.

In heaven, Indra was happy too. 'Now I know that creatures on earth can be truly grateful as well!' he said.

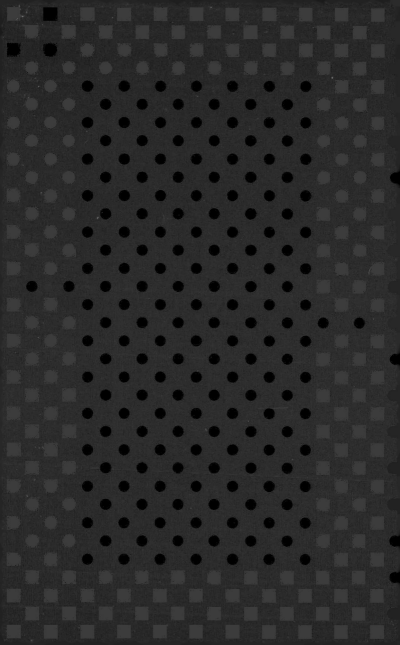